Motherfucking Sharks

Motherfucking Sharks

by Brian Allen Carr

A Lazy Fascist Western

Lazy Fascist Press
an imprint of Eraserhead Press
205 NE Bryant Street
Portland, Oregon 97211

www.lazyfascistpress.com

ISBN: 978-1-62105-123-7

Printed in the USA.

I

The streaked stranger showed a few days ahead of the storm, his body inked with indigenous-mannered images, his haul dragged by a one-eyed mule called Murm. The stranger went by Crick.

He carried a bouquet of roses ahead of him as though the flowers cast light and he traversed dark-stained wilderness, but the sun brightened all things the moment he arrived. Less than a day later, the great-orange orb seemed pulled behind blankets of gangrenous flesh, dead to the world that lay prone to the flood from the rain, but when Crick appeared he had to thin his eyes at the strength of life's shine.

He was a gentleman, Crick, and the flowers were gifts for the women of the town. Kindness was his heart, but the look of him was some awkward grind of tomfoolery and horror. His beast of burden dragged a wagon, the wagon brimming with harpoons and nets, and shambling behind the rickety wooden carriage, on tethers of varying lengths, were the naked jaws of sharks, their multitudes of teeth chipping and chirping along the rocks as Murm the mule dragged them. There was a music to it all, a sort of macabre waltz or a hysterical dirge. All percussion. All noise. Bloodcurdling. Amusing. Daffy. Absurd.

The township reluctantly welcomed him.

"What are you?" asked Mom, her skirt chalk blue and her eyes almost colorless. "You look wacky."

Crick handed her the flowers. "For you," he said. Then, "I'm a salesman." Crick looked back at the mountains he'd just dragged through, over a slow, gnarled path the shape of intestines. "You got trouble coming," he said. "Without what I've got," he continued, "you won't stand a chance."

A stub of a man leaned against the eave post of the porch Crick stood in the shade of, chewed some brown clot and drooled himself. "What kind of trouble we talking?" he asked.

Crick smiled. "Ever been to the ocean?"

Mom motioned to a lass with yellow hair who came skipping up silent and clutched the flowers away to find them water to be plopped away into. "Once," Mom said, "when I was a daughter to a drunk. We drove out there in an automobile and Dad fell asleep in the sun. His skin blistered and he couldn't sit for days. You see," she said, "he was naked and on his stomach when the sleep took him. I had to rub his ass with salve."

Crick nodded. "A sunburn is a mild malady for the ocean to bestow," he said. "You get in the water?" he asked.

"The water?" Mom said.

"And not just a toe."

Mom thought. "I did," she said. "I swam in it. The waves dragged over me, and I paddled along with them and was tossed in the currents." She smiled. "I got a sunburn too, but I'd the good sense to keep clothes on."

"You can't get in the water no more," Crick said. "It's infested with them."

The stubby man moved the clot from one cheek to the next with his tongue, the slurp sound of its moving the color of oysters. "Them what?" he asked.

Crick licked his lips. "When I was a boy I premonitioned it. My mom would take me to the gulf waters and have me play in the brown waves capped with white, the solution the consistency of a soup you'd never choose served to you, and the nightmares of the knowing what lurked in the murk of that non-translucent fluid filled me with terrors of violence to come upon me. Sharks," said Crick, "motherfucking sharks. Their eyes the shape of murderers' intentions and their mouths filled with these," Crick walked to the back of his wagon, and dragged a tether from hand to hand until he'd pulled a shark jaw into his grip, and he held it aloft for Mom to see. "Teeth," he said, "teeth as," he stuttered, "teeth as sharp as razor blades."

Mom eyed the jaw. "I don't follow," she said.

Crick clenched his free fist tight. "Motherfucking sharks," he said.

Again the man repositioned his mouthed clot, a lurching noise like a horse hoof in mud. "Strange a man who gives flowers then speaks that word," he dabbed brown drool from his chin, "in front of a lady."

"Bad words seem sweet compared to what I've seen," said Crick, "compared to what's headed your way."

Mom then stared at Crick as though his mind was awash with hallucinations. "I still," she said, "don't understand what threat you mean." She shook her head. "You've talked about oceans and you've talked about sharks, but we are days from the water, and I don't believe any of us had it in mind to travel that direction anyhow."

"Don't matter," said Crick. A satchel strap lay across his chest and he tugged it so the bag rested at his waist in front of him. He reached inside, and, as he did, the drool-stained man put his hand on the butt of his revolver, but he relaxed once Crick fished out the first skull. "This," said Crick, "was my mother." He fished another, "This my Pa." And another, "This my dear wife." Another still, "This my son." He had the four skulls rested in the crook of his left arm, cradling them against his belly so they stared out toward Mom.

She looked at them. "I'm sorry for your loss," she said, "but I'm still only confused."

"Ha," said Crick, "let me enlighten you," and in saying this, he shuffled two of the skulls into his right grip, and chucked one aloft, and then the next, and his left arm did the same, which surprised Mom, you could see in her face, and the man dabbed his drool again, and his eyes went wide, and in the background the noises of doors opening and closing and steps in the street as the several dozen townsfolk amassed to watch the wicked-featured stranger, streaked with lines, juggling skulls at the center of their town and screaming his hysterical tale of death and doom and dismemberment and catastrophe.

"I am not from the coast myself," said Crick, "I am from a valley. And it started with rain as it always does. It comes on winds that smell of blood, the storm that sweeps the motherfucking sharks from man-dwelling village to man-dwelling village, where they fall as . . . fall as rain, as spores in the drops, to land on the land, and emerge from the wetness," his speech stuttering every time the juggling became labored.

"These dastardly creatures are made to kill and fit with some magic that enables their swimming through the same air, the same air we now breathe." As he spoke, the skulls clapped Crick's hands in the juggling, the sound of bare feet dancing on tile to despicable tunes. "They've an unquenchable thirst for the, unquenchable thirst for the blood of man, and had I not been in a cage when they came for us, I'd not stand in front of you now.

"I was a magician before this, practicing a, practicing an escape. My wife had locked me inside a containment to be dropped into a pond. We'd been indoors for days waiting for torrential rains to abate, but the sun had, the sun had broke the storm and warmed the day for us to emerge in.

"My family watched on, anticipating my triumph at the new trick, and my son was just about to push the cage from the platform and into the waters below when the first shark sprang from the grubby puddles, its rage audible in its thrashing the atmosphere, and its wickedness like a hiss that filled your veins with fear.

"You've never known horror until you've watched your son's arms bitten from his body by a creature you felt certain could only exist in imagination, and felt the warmth of his red blood spray your skin as you rattled inside a cage incapable of coming to his aid."

Crick's juggling ceased, as he caught his son's skull in his right hand, held it aloft for the onlookers to ogle, and he cradled the other three skulls in his left arm.

"He screamed, 'Daddy!' his eyes wide, his upper half limbless, his skin paling as his life flooded from where his arms had once been." The juggling resumed. "And I forgot. Forgot all my tricks. Inside that cage, even at the bottom of the pond, I knew to take the ferreted key from my waistband and calmly unlock the containment, but faced that way with the, faced that way with the murder of my loves, I merely clenched my fists around those black-iron bars and pulled wildly, watching as my wife," again the juggling ceased, the wife's skull now on display above Crick, "had her tummy severed in one great chomp, her guts spilling from her like confetti that she tried to pack back into the place they'd once been, but of course that was useless." Again he juggled. "She heaped about in the gore as a multitude of mako sharks descended upon her, hiding their ravenous feeding from my eyes with their fins, bodies and tails.

"But my mother," the juggling stopped as the mother's skull was displayed, "was a quick bite for a great white," Crick juggled, "and I watched the whole of her disappear feet first into that giant monster, her face drawn into a blood-colored scream as he chomped down, and she screamed for my father," the father's skull was now showed its reverence as the juggling ceased, "who himself was taken by four hammerheads, each beast grabbing their own limb," the skulls were sent around, "and going in their own, going in their own direction, and he burst as a water-filled balloon may, the goop that filled him heaving from force in all directions as I cowered in my cage, closing my eyes as tight as I could to those horrors and plugging my ears with my fingers."

Crick stopped altogether and put the skulls back in his satchel. "Seemed to take an eternity for those sharks to give up on eating me. They rammed their heads into my cage and snarled their snarls until the sun dried them up again as vapor, and the storm that housed them moved along." Crick looked at the crowd of shocked faces. Then he pointed at the mountains in the distance. "That same storm is just on the other side of those peaks. Those same motherfucking sharks are coming for you," he said, and he pointed his right index finger at each individual in his presence.

The man who chewed the clot pulled it from his mouth and flung it to the ground, and it dragged like a comet through the dirt road, leaving a trail of brown yuck in its wake. He looked about from man to man in the crowd, each of their eyes laboring knowingly toward his own.

He nodded gently.

He gave the signal.

They descended upon Crick, driving him to the earth and pulling his arms behind his back, and he could only fight feebly as they cuffed him.

They stood him up.

"Sorry for this," Mom said to him. "But here, we lock the crazies away."

The men of the town dragged Crick toward the jailhouse, his legs kicking as his body scuffed over the street, the dirt dusting his pant legs which drew forward against their will.

"You'll regret," he screamed as they arrested him, "you'll regret what," he screamed, "you'll regret what you've done."

The man packed a fresh chew and chewed it into place. He looked at Mom. "The mule?" he said.

Mom looked at Murm, at his single eye and ragged body. "Doesn't look like a working mule," she said. "I suppose," she continued, "we should down him."

The man eyed the mule as well, and he nodded thoughtfully, showing approval. "Fair enough," said the man. Then he gave another signal.

Two odd-looking brothers came to take the mule away.

II

This is the shark: a blood-hungry thing, utterly addicted—a machine made to hunt the thing it desires.

You aren't much different.

If a human is a molar, the shark is a fang, but both creatures are just instruments the mouth of the world uses to chew its prey. The shark hunts in bursts and bites, the human hunts in endless stroll. Forward, the shark screams. Forward, mutters the human.

Most likely, this is for several reasons:

1. Sharks must swim to breathe; humans can sleep and snore.

2. Humans can hold what they desire in their hands and contemplate it; a shark must hold everything in its mouth, out of sight.

3. Sharks do not blink, their eyes stay open. To them, everything is either there or gone. Humans can hold something in their hands, behind their back while their eyes are closed, and know where it is. Because of this, humans have the luxury of being less absolute—their perception of existence working in increments—so their addiction seems less constant.

It is a trick of perception.

The shark labors only in the physical world, while the human schemes in the universe of its mind. The shark is a murderer, but it's an honest one. It is killing you, or you are alive. The human can kill you a million times in its imagination while pouring you a glass of water. If you don't believe me, get a job waiting tables. Contemplate how many murders you plot while hurrying to gather customers their food.

Here is the future and the plight of that world: Crick is in a jail cell, and Murm is being led away by executioners.

The next town over is beset by motherfucking sharks.

Two identical twins have holed up in a barn, the sole survivors of the town. Her name is Tilly; his name is Tim. They've cotton-colored skin and eyes the shade of sorghum fields when gazed at from a distance. His hands, tight as sun-dried clay. Her hands, smooth as sunflower petals. Fear holds them both in its sinister grip, their hearts haphazardly pumping in their chests in sporadic fashion, metaphorical loose stones down a mortality-shaped hillside.

They can hear the gray-bodied sharks bouncing against the broad, red walls of the barn they've sought refuge in. They hunker in the loose hay, trying to quell their possessed breathing, the stale stench of the feed and straw sits thick in their throats, and their ears flitter with the music of splintering wood and nails and screws singing loose from their sockets.

"What do we do?" Tilly asks.

"We'll die here," says Tim, a resigned sheet of panic making milky his eyes. "Just you and me."

Outside the sun dries the wet of the world back toward the medicinal blue of heaven's expanse, begging the land away from its state of recent flooding, and shivers of sharks swim rampant through the trees and streets gone red with the spilled human blood. Crimson drops bloom oddly through the murky rain puddles the color of caramel. Skeletons sit ramshackle in queer repose, spare bits of sinew cling to the bones being picked over by courageous carrion birds that the sharks seem only remotely interested in. It is an odd jury indeed that has descended upon the town to cast its un-uttered but obvious verdict. It's a simple sentencing really: Pure, imperfect death.

On the day their town came under siege, the citizens had flocked to the square to witness Tim's hanging. He'd been found guilty of horse thievery, and had been ordered hanged the day the rains came, his execution postponed by the inclement weather. Tim didn't mind. He sat in his cell drawing nude breasts on butcher paper with a charcoal pencil.

"You've a sick mind," the sheriff's deputy had told him as he ogled Tim's artwork through the bars of his confinement, "but," he said clicking his tongue, widening his eyes, "a damn steady hand."

Tim touched the side of his head, "All from in here," he said, "pure imagination."

The sheriff's deputy tilted his head in thought. "Whatcha mean, boy?"

Tim, who'd been busy shading out breasts, lowered his pencil to the page. "I ain't never been with no woman," he said.

"Never?" said the sheriff's deputy.

"Not a once," Tim said.

Outside the rain sheeted heavy against the roof, spilling through the gutters in belches and slurps. Thunder crashed righteously, and the skies strobed with lightning.

"Hell," said the sheriff's deputy, "if it weren't raining like this," he moved to a window and drew a curtain away with the back of a hand, "I'd score a whore for you myself."

"Maybe when it stops?" said Tim, and he jumped to his feet and clenched the cell bars in his grip. "Just quick like?"

The sheriff's deputy looked at him sadly. "We'll see," he said, and of course, nothing came of it.

The morning the sun broke through on the storm, the sheriff's deputy stood on the gallows with a mask over his face, and the sheriff fetched Tim from the cell himself, on account of all the commotion.

"Some people," said the sheriff, "don't wanna see you hanged, but I'm not one of them."

"Yessir," Tim said.

"You're young," said the sheriff, "but you are guilty."

After they dropped the noose around his neck, the sheriff asked Tim if he had anything to say.

He nodded, his body trembling, his skin paled by fear, eyes red at the edges.

"I took a horse," he said. "A nag," he continued, "to eat on. Y'all knew my pa, how he disappeared in a manner mysterious, and how my sister and I've struggled in his absence. Look at me," he said, looking down at his thin frame, "I'm near bones from hunger."

"Thief," cried someone from the crowd, then another hollered, "Hang 'em."

"Fine," yelled Tim. "Hang me till I'm dead. You're gonna do it, I know. I don't appeal for your change of heart. I don't appeal to your sympathies in that regard, to look back at your histories with my family and find in those friendships evidence to implore you to turn the other cheek, to take the noose from my neck and allow me to walk free," Tim looked down at the platform he stood on. "But there's one thing I do ask," he said, "and I ask it in earnest.

"I'm a young man," he continued. "And, aside from horse theft, I've lived a pure life."

The crowd was silent. If you knew what to listen for, you could have heard it—the sharks rising slowly from the puddles that glimmered in the sunlight. As it was, the crowd was oblivious, their attentions solely on the last words of Tim.

"On account of my pureness," said Tim. "I have never known a woman."

An odd shock took the crowd.

"I've never even seen one's form fully disrobed."

Whispers from the crowd at the oddity of Tim's statements came bundling up.

"I'm just asking for a glimpse," said Tim and he looked down from woman to woman, "just show me your body," he said, "you don't gotta let me feel nothing, just lemme look."

"Boy's a pervert," someone in the crowd yelled, and laughter filled the square, and the sheriff dropped a black bag over Tim's head, and Tim started screaming.

"Just lemme see," he hollered, his voice muted by the bag, "just a glimpse," he yelled again. "Just some titties," he pleaded, "not even everything."

A scream came from the edge of the crowd. A shriek the color of death. A thing jagged to the ears, so coarse that the whole town turned to see the commotion, the shape of which was so impractical that it didn't initially register in their eyes. Gray figures thrashed violently and drops of blood flung from the shrieking body of the screamer much as water scatters from a wet, shagging dog.

"Jail break," hollered the sheriff, who assumed what was being witnessed was some posse amassed to try and rescue the condemned, and he signaled his deputy to drop the hatch on the prisoner, which he did.

The trapdoor opened, and Tim tugged toward the earth, but, just as he fell, a shoal of tiger sharks descended like fists upon the platform, shattering the gallows that the rope was tied around, splintering wood in every conceivable direction, and Tim dropped to the soft earth and landed face first in a puddle with his hands tied behind him. In the dark, he did not see, but he could hear the screaming and it confused him.

What did he build then in his mind? The mind of such pristine imagination? The mind that made nude breasts emerge from the clothes they'd always hid behind? We'll never know. But it is inconceivable that he envisioned what truly transpired.

Allow yourself to see this slowly.

A town of dirt roads, all roads leading to a square.

At the center of the square, a gallows.

Surrounding the gallows, standing on swollen grass made magically green by the recent rains, dressed in clothes of bandaged fabric, thread thin from near constant wear and colors faded from hand-washing, sun drying, a scant hundred citizens, their faces lustful with the anticipation of witnessing a thief's death by hanging, loitering unaware of the miserable fate about to befall them.

This town—the buildings constructed from rescued and forgotten timber, patched together with twice-used nails and painted with colors stumbled upon in discovered paint buckets, seemingly erected by wayward carnival folks who'd grown wearisome of entertaining and had decided to root themselves where the fatigue toward their occupation became unbearable—is ill-equipped for any attack, let alone an impossible one.

Imagine one hundred sharks springing from the edges of puddles the way mushrooms blossom from dung heaps when watched at high speed.

If witnessed in actuality, you wouldn't believe it.

Some things go so against the line of logic we've branded hot on our brains, that their impressions on our minds echo with madness and are rejected, spat away, and even if you look twice you still don't believe it.

Many members in that crowd actually walked toward the

sharks that had emerged with their hands out in front of them in hopes of touching away the apparitions that had gathered, because when the world appears insane to us, we trust touch more than sight.

For this reason, several from the crowd quickly lost limbs, and, "My arm, my arm," was the first curse hollered in English—not just the noises of death that erupted from the throats of those screaming.

Let us watch from high above the choreography of the sharks as they circle the hanging's crowd pushing the would-be onlookers further inward toward a clump of struggling men, women and children ferocious with fear and dizzy with their thwarted attempts at fleeing.

Any soul who moves toward the perimeter of the square is met with myriad sharks circling in opposite directions, and, in this way, the sharks are able to corral the entirety of the crowd in mere moments.

Great whites and makos and tigers and bonnets and lemons and nurses and threshers and blacknose and blacktips and spinners and bull sharks and duskys and finetooths and smalltails and silkies and dogfish and hammerheads, sharpnose, and browns. All circling, circling, circling their death-patterned courses, pushing the mass of horror-stricken humans deeper into their clump of false-security safety-in-numbers, huddling together with their backs to the murderous fish that had somehow stripped away order from the universe and learned to navigate against the laws of the physical world.

Have you ever seen a thing the first time and known its name?

These were the motherfucking sharks.

And the name of them came cackling up from the mass of terror-stricken crowd members who, though moments before stood with eyes glistening toward the gallows, mouths watering for the thief to be dropped and dangled by the noose until dead, recognized now in the eyes of their encroachers the same glistening premonition of a death to be witnessed and swelled with apprehension, their spastic bodies floundering toward the nucleus of their pile, the weight of those out toward the crust of the lump of them crushing and suffocating those trapped in the core.

Once contained, paralyzed by the quagmire birthed by their instinct of flight, the sharks began to plunge against those at the edges, tearing bodies in swift jabs, their felony-sharp teeth exposed in their draped-open mouths, and the sharks merely had to swim their death orifices against their victims, plucking away mouthfuls from the clump of them at random.

But what of the hooded Tim?

Last seen, he lay bound and blinded from the slaughter transpiring, a limp noose around his neck.

Indeed, a frail rescue attempt was worked out for him.

His sister, his twin, had set to it even before her brother's guilty verdict had been announced, because she'd lived long enough in that town to know that those who dwelled there would always disappoint her, and she'd prayed thanks to God when the rains came, because without them, her fragmentary draft toward his rescue could only be dreamed over.

Sadly, her plan was only a first step. It involved tunneling.

From the ramshackle red barn that housed the community dry storage, Tilly dug each night a portion of passage from the dirt floor of that building to the shadow of the gallows.

The night before Tim's original execution date, Tilly wept in the tunnel as she worked her shovel, well aware that her efforts would fall short, and, come break of day, there'd exist still several feet of dirt between the subterranean channel she'd slaved over and the spot in the earth where she'd hoped the tunnel would emerge.

Tilly labored alone.

She trusted that several of her friends and family members would lend assistance if asked; however, she did not trust that any one of them would be able to keep the endeavor secret until the thing's completion.

She had to rescue Tim in private, unassisted, and she struggled herself delirious in the solitary scramble of the chore. During the last several feet of the undertaking she heard phantom voices casting whispers through her imagination and saw invented, colorful explosions smearing through the hovel's dark quarters. She broke ground mere seconds after her brother dropped to the earth—the sharks' attack being infinitely fortuitous in this regard, because without it, she would have merely managed to emerge from the dirt in time to see her brother's death. As it was, in the hysteria of the odd attack transpiring, Tilly was given the perfect diversion under which to operate. The only flaw to the sharks' presence was, for several moments, Tilly assumed she'd ground herself into utter insanity, and that what she saw—the phantasmagorical sharks hunting human prey—was mere illusion.

Either way, she was able to extract her hooded twin from the scene of it, tugging his ankles until he tumbled into her tunnel where she unhooded and unbound him.

Tim did not understand how, but he was safe, and the two twins crawled to the red barn where they barricaded the tunnel as Tilly explained the shark attack to her brother.

"Impossible," he told her.

She shook her head, "It's true."

They found a hole in the barn wall that faced the town square, and they took turns watching as the shark army minced the men, women and children of the town, tossing the bits and pieces of them like wet rags that sprayed hot blood as they flung to and fro, and they did their best to keep quiet in the full-fledged terror of their witnessing it.

"What happens," said Tilly, "when they're done with all them?"

It is a myth that sharks can smell fear, but they can sense panic, and, as the sharks undid the troop of townsfolk—making them first merely dead and then muck and then bones—the twins' hearts heaved and raced, and their breaths hurried.

Let this be now in your mind—Tim and Tilly in the hay. They've cotton-colored skin and eyes the shade of sorghum fields when gazed at from a distance. His hands, tight as sun-dried clay. Her hands, smooth as sunflower petals. Fear holds them both in its sinister grip, their hearts haphazardly pumping in their chests in sporadic fashion, metaphorical loose stones down a mortality-shaped hillside.

They can hear the gray-bodied sharks bouncing against the broad, red walls of the barn they've sought refuge in. They hunker in the loose hay, trying to quell their possessed breathing, the stale stench of the feed and straw sits thick in their throats, and their ears flitter with the music of splintering wood and nails and screws singing loose from their sockets.

"What do we do?" Tilly asks.

"We'll die here," says Tim, a resigned sheet of panic making milky his eyes. "Just you and me." He drags his hand through his hair. The sharks are splintering through. "I'm gonna say something," Tim says, "you might not want to hear," he continues, "I almost died today," he takes his twin's hands, "a virgin," he says.

Tilly does not like the look in his eyes. She pulls back her hands. The sharks thudding is like thunder.

"Listen," says Tim, "we're our only option."

The world becomes silent to Tilly. "What are you saying?" she asks. Her mind flitters with memories of her growing up alongside Timmy—her identical in every way except in their sex—and all the things they'd done that did not lead them to this. There were times they'd lay in each other's arms on warm summer nights watching the night sky for comets and listening to the music of crickets, the black of the sky's endlessness draped over them like a blanket, but in that there was no echo of anything beyond sibling affection, though in this new language her brother speaks—a disgusting and twisted English that suggests an occurrence repulsive to her—that old memory seems crippled and twisted, and the dross of Timmy's nature cleaves at the pure parts of him that Tilly has kept in her heart. "What are you saying?" she asks.

"I've never thought it before now," Timmy says, "but inside me there's rage toward the idea of dying without knowing." A wall breaks open and light spills through at them, and in that light they can see a murderous shark's myriad teeth striking wildly at the boards of the barn.

Tilly thinks a time when her brother and she shared a slice of watermelon while sitting naked in a bathtub. They were six or seven. The pink juice of the fruit ran down their chins and into the water.

"Maybe boys and girls are different that way," says Tim, "because I can see that you're not thinking the same."

Now the shark has worked his body into the gape in the barn, his head thrashing, eyes locked on Tilly and Tim.

"But," says Timmy, "I'd do anything for you."

Tilly nods. It is true. Half the reason she'd tunneled to his rescue is because of all the good he'd done her. The horse he'd stolen was on her behalf. He could have left her when their father died and stomped off into the world and into a safer life, but he'd stayed to make sure she was cared for, though she cared for him in turn. Hadn't she mended his clothes and cooked him dinner, and placed cool rags on his forehead when he took ill with flu, and read to him from the Bible while he fever dreamed so he wouldn't catch nightmares, and hadn't she brought him to this barn? So, he'd asked for more.

Tilly sees two clear anxieties working inside of Tim. She

sees his fear of death, and she sees the sexual anticipation. She looks at his face, identical to her own but with shorter hair. A soft skin. A smooth form.

She places her hands near his throat. She nods. She runs her hands down his shirt unfastening the buttons. The dirtied cotton falls open. Timmy's chest heaves up and down. The sharks make murder noises. The barn cracks further open. Tilly takes to her own shirt. She spreads it open revealing her soft breast, and Tim touches clumsily at her nipples, lifting the softness of her form, and he lowers his face to her and suckles, licking the dark pink areola shiny with his tongue. He drags his mouth down her smooth stomach, licking away the salty slick of her sweat, and he hoists her skirt to her thighs, and his hands dive between her legs, and he feels the wet of her as he spreads her legs open, and he trembles at the warmth. Tilly breathes nervously and unbuttons Timmy's pants, and drapes them from him, her hands running across his buttocks, and his cock springs up at her, and she wraps her legs around him, and grabs him, guiding it into her. Timmy's face goes slack as he pushes himself through her moistness, and they both whimper unknowingly, and the sharks are chomping a bad-murder music and the light builds as the barn breaks further open, and Timmy lunges into her with all the awkwardness of the universe, and they roll back into the hay, and he lifts himself up and stares down at his twin, and both of their faces grimace with sex pains and horror and longing and shame, and they are both lost in that music of each other, in that wild endless energy of the coming finale, as though all of them is a spitting whisper shot through a vacuum and aimed at eternity.

Then the sharks are upon them.

III

Bark and Scraw were tasked with Murm's execution. They led him down the main road toward their workshop where the two brothers served as butchers, barbers, and doctors to the town. They could not heal you. Most of their visitors were so near death, they couldn't fight their being dragged there. Going to see Bark and Scraw was synonymous with the end, but Murm didn't know this. He walked one-eyed, being dragged by the rope around his neck.

Of the two, Scraw was slower—mentally and physically. He walked alongside Murm and watched the mule's face as they progressed.

"Is this a boy mule?" asked Scraw, "or a girl mule?"

Bark, who pulled the rope a few steps ahead of them, looked back, sneered. "There's only boy mules, idiot," he said, and he leaned harder on the rope.

"Huh," said Scraw.

A silence passed—only the sounds of Murm's heavy breathing and hooves against the dirt.

Bark looked back again, watched Scraw smiling at the mule.

Bark stopped. The rope went slack in his hand as Murm took another few steps before halting.

"Why do you ask?" said Bark as he looked now at his brother's goofiness toward the animal.

Scraw pet Murm's mane. "No reason," he said. "Just curious."

Bark seemed to sniff at his brother, trying to discern a veiled intention.

Both brothers had peculiar features, but, of the two, Bark seemed further human. Their lips hung loose and their eyes seemed pulled back on their heads and their skin seemed dirt-stained even after they'd bathed and their hairlines were high. It was as if you had no choice but to contemplate them through a convex and dirty lens, and their heads twitched slightly every time they talked.

"Nah," said Bark, "there's something to it." He grabbed at Scraw's shirt. "Gum it out. What's in your silly head?"

Scraw gazed at the dirt, then up at his brother. "He keeps winking at me," he said.

Bark's mouth gaped open. "If we'd different mothers," Bark said, "I'd call you a dumb sonofabitch," he said, and he grabbed Murm by the jaw and showed Scraw again how Murm was missing an eye. "All this damned beast does is wink," he said, "at everything." He let the mule go. "What's a wink?" he asked.

"Huh?" said Scraw.

"A wink, you dumb sonofabitch," Bark said, "what is it?"

The sun hung low in the west, and Scraw looked away and saw thick clouds the color of ocean gathering above the mountains in the east. The snow-capped peaks appeared incapably white against the deep-dark backdrop.

Scraw closed an eye and raised a thumb and the tallest white peak disappeared behind his fingernail. Then, "Closing one eye," he said.

"That's right," said Bark, "closing an eye," he continued, "so this mule don't blink, it just winks, and you're just standing on his eye side, so it just seems he's winking at you."

Scraw lowered his thumb, opened both eyes and looked at his brother. "Nah," he said. "I think there's more to it."

"More to it?" said Bark. "More to it?" He turned then and walked forward, pulling the rope. "What more could there be?"

Scraw sighed. "Hard telling," he said, "for certain."

They got to the workshop and raised the door on its rails, the door squealing as the runners rode the rusty tracks and the door tucked up against the ceiling. Murm spooked a bit when they brought him in, presumably because he could smell the blood of prior deaths, but Scraw petted his mane gently and cooed him back to calm. "See," said Scraw to Bark, "I've got a way with him," he ran his hand down Murm's back, "he likes me."

Bark looked at his brother and felt sick at his closeness to the mule. "It doesn't matter," said Bark. "The thing will be dead soon."

Scraw nodded. "I guess," he said.

Bark grabbed an axe off the wall. "No," he said. "There's no guessing to it. It's our obligation to make it so. It is in our job description that when we're asked to slaughter we slaughter. It is not in our job description to discern the intention behind the winks of mules or to spot something larger in the fabric of our ability to soothe a mule out of a panic sparked by the stench of old deaths." Bark took the axe to a sharpening stone, worked the edge of the blade against it. "You're soft toward animals," he said, "and while I don't wholly understand it, I'm sympathetic to your condition, because I grew up watching you follow sheep into the field and naming the breakfast eggs before you cracked 'em," he said, "and I feel sorry for you, in some fashion, because you've that heart inside you and this job as your livelihood, but I do believe, in the core of me I swear it, that much of the lamentation you're forced into is because of behaviors you've decided on for yourself, and I further believe, again from my center, that you could just as easily decide from the get go 'this is a mule, a stupid mule, and I'm going to kill it, and that I don't care if it does wink at me, or if I can calm it, because killing the thing is my job.'" Bark finished sharpening the axe blade, and he raised the axe to his brother. Scraw just looked at the wooden handle of it, worn smooth from use and stained away from its original pine shade by bloodshed. "Take it," said Bark. "Don't make me angry at you."

Scraw ran his hand up and down Murm's back. He put his nose close to the animal's mane and breathed deeply the acrid smell of the animal. He looked in his brother's eyes. "I don't know," he said, "I don't believe I'm able."

Those unfamiliar with the siblings might've witnessed this dispute as an indication of each respective brother's role in their collective endeavors as butcher, barbers, and doctors to the town; however, the evidence emerging from the conflict would prove mildly misleading, as the natures of the brothers' services in day to day proceedings were divided along far less virtuous lines. It was not: Bark the butcher and Scraw the healer. It was: Bark the doer and Scraw the porter. That is to say: Bark butchered, slaughtered, attempted to heal, and gave haircuts. Scraw cleaned, cooked, and kept house. He ran errands. He took notes.

If the task was pedestrian, it belonged to Scraw. If the task bared some significance and affected some manner of drastic, perceptible change, it was Bark's.

This was not the first time Bark had attempted to bestow a fraction of his duties onto his brother in an attempt to cure his deep-seated sensitivities; however, this was the first time that Bark had ventured to press Scraw to go so far as kill. Prior experiments in this regard were confined to ridding Scraw of his aversion to cutting hair or fabricating meat—all things, in Bark's opinion, that seemed easy even for the most genteel characters to execute, but Scraw was averse to these actions.

"I get nauseous at the sound of the scissors," he had told Bark, and when Bark would cut Scraw's hair, Scraw would plug his ears with his fingers.

As for parceling beef or venison or bison or birds, Scraw didn't offer up reasons. He merely kept his fists clenched and said, "No," when offered the butchering blade.

"You can cook it," said Bark. "What's the difference?"

But Scraw just shook his head, said, "I can't explain it."

Here, however, was a much further campaign with the aim of mending Scraw's defective character.

"Take the axe, Scraw," Bark said, his whole form clenching with annoyance at his brother's reluctance.

It had been some years since Bark had grown irritated enough at his brother to render harm to his person, but Scraw saw in his current posture some echo of the fury which had preceded the last violence visited to him at Bark's hands, and, with a reluctance unfathomable, an electric hesitation that seemed to skip on his bones, Scraw let his trembling hand extend toward the implement of slaughter, but, as soon as the wooden handle stroked the skin of his fingers, he pulled the hand back and hid his face with it and whimpered, "I can't."

Then, the oddest thing transpired. Scraw looked down into Murm's eye, and he saw in it, against the black ball in the socket, first himself reflected and then a future. It was opaque, the prospect imaged there, but what the vision lacked in clarity of specifics it made up for in certainty of promise, and Scraw understood everything even before the mule winked again, before the animal let his eyelids fade gently closed then open back imploringly at him, and Scraw knew what he had to do even before Bark yelled at him.

"You're a goddamned. . ."

"Wait," said Scraw, and he reached his hand out for the axe.

This disorganized Bark's operation and he stammered out a bald reaction, stating plainly, "Huh?"

"Give it here," said Scraw. "Give me the axe."

Bizarrely, a sort of defeated look glossed over Bark's eyes, and, when the axe was gone from his grip, he appeared deflated. Perhaps he'd grown so accustomed to his brother's resistance his form had distended with it, and now, with the hindrance removed, the puss of that swelling leaked out in the world, and the action skinnied him. "You certain?" Bark asked. "You can do this?" he said, but Scraw just hefted the axe over his shoulder and turned his back toward Bark.

Scraw looked down then at Murm. He waited. The brown mule raised his face at him. He waited. The brown mule turned his cheek. He waited. It came again. The mule, for certain, bared his one eye full at Scraw, and, with all the intention that any being could have behind any performance pre-meditated, the mule winked.

Scraw swung then.

He packed all his might into a single swing, the axe racing off his shoulder, slashing its path just over the mule's head, and Scraw rolled his shoulders to face his brother's frame.

Bark's eyes went wide as the axe head whipped around, the blade of the tool torpedoing in a direct line for his chest, where the newly sharpened implement thwacked a burial for itself, the axe mashing Bark's heart back to its handle, and Bark stepped back as Scraw let go and watched Bark grab haphazardly at where he was gotten several times before his legs gave from shock or death, and Bark fell to the ground in a bloody heap.

IV

Crick learned the man who chewed and spat, the man who'd sent the signal resulting in his capture, went by Kinky Pete, and at that knowledge Crick laughed and bit his thumb.

"Strangers often find that amusing," Kinky Pete told him, "but it's on account of my spine." Pete unbuttoned his flannel shirt and let the smooth fabric drape off his shoulders, and he turned so Crick could see the gnarled backbone that swerved and twisted down away from his skull. "If it were straight," Pete said buttoning up, "I'd be a half foot taller than I am."

Crick was locked in one of two cells in the miniature jailhouse adjacent the sheriff's offices. "Ifs are just wishes we should keep to ourselves," said Crick.

"Ah," said Kinky Pete, "you're just sore we got you put away," he said, "but remember," he continued, "it's for your own safety."

Crick eyed the black bars of his cage. He gripped two in his hands and pulled back and the cell didn't as much as rattle. He put his hands to his face and sniffed the metallic odor left behind on his palms and went to his bunk, slunk down on its hardness, said calmly, "It's not my safety I'm concerned with."

"Right," said Kinky Pete, "the. . ." Pete scratched his head, "what did you call them?"

"The mother, mother, mother," stuttered Crick, "motherfucking sharks."

"Of course," said Pete. He rolled his eyes and then there was a knock at the door.

Pete went to it and opened it up.

It was Scraw delivering mule stew for the prisoners.

"How many you got?" Scraw asked.

"Just the one," answered Kinky Pete, and he took from Scraw a pie plate of stew covered with a scrap of flour sack and a brown paper bag of cornbread hunks, and he turned with the vittles and walked them to Crick's cell, slid the pie plate beneath the slot in the cage door saying, "mule stew," and dropped the cornbread through the bars saying, "bread."

Crick nodded, asked, "Mule stew?"

Kinky Pete nodded, answered, "Yup, your mule."

Crick stood and walked to the bag, picked it up and looked inside. He took up the pie plate.

"We had the thing slaughtered and cooked up good for you," said Kinky Pete.

Crick folded back a corner of the flour sack and sniffed at the stew. "Hm," said Crick, "that's not mule."

By now Scraw was gone, but Kinky Pete looked at the door and pointed. "Just ask Scraw next time he's around," Pete said, "it's mule. Your mule. Your-mule stew."

Crick packed a spoonful of stew into his drawn-open mouth, chewed slackly, said, "I've had mule," said, "this is not that."

Kinky Pete turned angry, "You calling me liar?" he asked.

"Or merely misinformed," said Crick.

"I'm neither thing," said Pete, "and won't be called such by a crazy man."

Crick took another bite, "And what," he asked, "makes you assume," he chewed, "I'm crazy?"

"To begin with," said Pete, "the look of you." Pete washed his gaze over the captive. "You're inked up and threadbare and ghastly and unbathed."

Crick swallowed. "I'm dirty," he said, "I've tattoos," he continued, "but that's not a sign of insanity."

"Well," said Pete, "the talk you talk, then."

"The talk I talk?"

"Sure. You tell stories unnatural that could only be strained out of the mind of a madman, and the manner in which you travel and present yourself, and how you juggle these," Pete walked to the wall where Crick's satchel hung on a peg, and he reached into it and retrieved a skull, which he held eyes-out toward Crick, "and that is madness."

Crick nodded, "Still," he said taking a hunk of crumbly cornbread and running it through the stew, "this is not mule. And thus, you're a liar. Or, misinformed."

"I'll not have it," said Pete.

"Liar," said Crick.

"I won't take it," said Pete.

And Crick said, "Misinformed."

Pete's face grew truly nasty at the taunting. He raised the skull above his head as though to slam it to the cement ground, shattering it. "Call it mule," he said.

"Can't do it," said Crick.

"Call it mule, or else."

"I was taught to never lie," and he smiled in a grained-toothed manner at Kinky Pete.

"Fine," said Pete, and he rushed the skull-holding hand at the ground with all his might, the strength of the whole endeavor apparent in his wicked-upped eyes, and he drove the gray human cranium into the ground with a smack that sent shards in several directions, and the chipped-up bone chunk jumped in a ricochet and clipped Pete's cheek with such force that the skin struck split open and coughed out a stream of hot-red blood that spilled swift down his face, and Pete covered up the gash with the same hand that had done the throwing, and he barked out some unintelligible language of anguish, and then he looked up at Crick.

Crick stayed calm. "Looks like that smarts," he said, pointing with the spoon.

Pete said nothing. Shock is the surest way to sew shut a proud mouth.

He kept his hand clasped to his face.

He ran out the jail, the whimper of him softly audible over his brisk-thrown steps.

The battered bit of skull that scraped off Pete had rolled against the cage bars, and Crick snagged it up and pulled the broken half of it into his cell. He knew which skull it was when Pete had showed him the eyes. Any of the other skulls would have forced him to say 'mule.' But, among the skulls he carried, this one was false. In theory, it belonged to his son, but, in truth, he had no idea whose it was. It was a stray thing he'd picked out of a shark-destroyed dwelling, and not even the original one at that. The first one he'd used in the stead of his son's had been long since thrown at an annoying woodpecker. The second, he'd given to a whore. He couldn't remember if this was the third or not.

Crick did not like to think deeply on his two days in captivity in the tiny cage the sharks kept him penned in, but every so often an event forced him back there.

The flavor of murder washed his present-moment eyes black, and the colors of that hideous memory pulled him back into the sick sea wherein he witnessed his family's mutilation— the tide of his misery drawing him down toward abyss.

Into the cage and the family and the day warm and the day warm humid and the sound of day like light like dust and into the cage the tight bars cutting soft shade from the dullard sun and the sound of mom and the sound of dad and wife and son and the sound of 'good luck, you can do it' and the sound of 'when I say when' and the sound of 'when I say when push the cage' and the sound of into the cage, the lock, and the sound of the lock clipping locked and the sound of into the cage and the day, and the 'you can do it, got the key?' and the son's face and the eyes the eyes of the son the blue the blue gray bright day sound of the eyes in the day and the sound of the son just about to press his weight on the cage and the thought of the, 'I'm about to fall' and the thought of 'will I pull it off?' and the sound of the remembering in that remembering of how the trick should work and the sound of how the thing would go or not go and the thoughts in that thought of the thought of 'what if?' and that thought of 'what then?' but the thought then of the form in the mind impossible, the thought of the beast appearing and the thought of the 'how could it be so?'

And then blood blood

Blood
And then screams screams
Screams
AND
The sound of the motherfucking sharks and the sound of
the motherfucking sharks and the sound of
the motherfucking sharks and
the sound of THE
motherfucking
sharks
!

Let us hold now in our minds the image of a man and a boy. The man is Crick, but not the Crick of now or then but the Crick of before we've ever seen him. The boy is his child and he is one and a half and he has just said his first word and that first word is 'Daddy.' The shape of this word slipping from the tongue of his son puffed Crick with pride, though he'd never imagined the word being associated with him. As a young man, his proclivity toward wayward schemes left the impression on most of those who chanced upon his presence that Crick would one day die wildly and alone, most likely with dirty clothes on. But Crick's wife—who he met on a riverboat in a romantic entanglement that included drinks with mint as a principal ingredient and porch-colored music played by a blind man with sass—possessed a demeanor that soothed Crick away from debauchery and toward domestication, and since first trading the phrase 'I love you' with her, the path of his activities bent away from the wicked. His son's birth seemed the natural conclusion to anything sordid in his nature, but the boy's first word being 'Daddy' seemed to further cement Crick's utter rehabilitation.

Crick was a decent man, even if he did still practice magic.

Before the wife, before the boy, Crick used his sleight of hand proficiency as an apparatus toward quackery, his magic just a method toward charlatanism and deception.

Simply put, he stole.

He was one of those troubling characters who could glance against you in a crowd and take your watch and wallet, spectacles and keys, but his charm also enabled in him larger, more blatant heists. He might come to your door selling religious texts and make away with the family piano as a donation toward an orphanage that never existed, and he'd sell the instrument to a friend of yours for a fraction of its worth, and you'd see it months later at a dinner party and question its origins, and the line of query would lead to the revelation that you'd been swindled and suckered by a man you'd thought sincere.

Family had taken that from him.

Daddy. The word daddy.

If it's never been aimed at you, you don't know its worth.

Diotima told Socrates, in his quest to understand love, that "the mortal nature is seeking as far as is possible to be everlasting and immortal: and this is only to be attained by generation, because generation always leaves behind a new existence in the place of the old," and so if you're ever called daddy, you become a kind of god, because the attribution of the word to your being is testament to the notion that some shadow of your existence cast by the light of time will stretch into the future and echo toward eternity.

Hold now in your mind two moments:

1. Crick being made immortal by his son calling him daddy.

2. That immortality's bloody revocation when the mother-fucking sharks descended upon his son.

And remember both events played out for Crick to witness, and know that the juxtaposition of events in the fold of Crick's mind crashed him toward devastation.

Let us now think of Crick in the cage while his family's devoured. He can do nothing but watch or try not to watch. He can do nothing but listen or try not to listen. The smell of blood and rain puddles thickens the air, and the sun stains Crick's skin as the sharks swim around him.

Sharks ram the cage fruitlessly, their mouths sprawled open to reveal teeth stained by the blood of Crick's loved ones. Their wicked, vacant eyes lock with Crick's. They thrash their bodies as they swim through the air.

Slowly, Crick watches as the sharks' forms pale away. Over the course of his two-day captivity, he sees their skins go transparent so the veins of them are visible, their cartilaginous skeletal systems apparent, and then they can be seen through like wax paper and then they lessen further until they're no more.

Once gone entirely, Crick pulls the cage key from his waistband and unlocks his entrapment, and he weeps his way from skeleton to skeleton, picking up skulls and holding them to his face.

But, a skeleton is gone.

On the ground, beside the cage, he finds the bones of his boy's arms, scattered haphazardly, the fingers of both hands jumbled together, but that is all.

The absence of the skeleton births a quest.

Let us now envision Crick as the wanderer he becomes.

Initially, he is not as our first encounter with him. He is not a streaked stranger inked with indigenous-mannered images.

He does not travel with a one-eyed mule. He does not haul harpoons from town to town and profess the coming onslaught of motherfucking sharks. He is less the ancient mariner and more Rapunzel's fallen prince. He bears no warning of things to come, he merely asks the questions as he progresses, "Have you seen an armless boy?"

An armless boy? An armless boy?

Crick crashes his way from town to town eating slop from trash cans and prickly pears foraged from cactus paddles.

An armless boy? An armless boy?

His history plagues him.

An armless boy? An armless boy?

"You look familiar," some say.

Armless boy?

"Didn't you make off with my piano?"

Armless?

"Tell us again about the orphans?"

Boy?

The nature of his twisted experience is made further unbelievable by the fact that his wake is burdened with falsities espoused.

"Sure, sure," most people say, "motherfucking sharks. Armless boy." They shake their heads. "Get to the point," they tell him, "what are you trying to take me for?"

Still, there are whispers. "A carnival. A freak show. A circus act. Some strangers."

Crick gathers shards of stories and crumples them together in his mind. "There was a boy. The boy was armless." And Crick follows any line offered him from place to place through miserable weather and over lands shunned by God.

In some towns, his reputation is so badgered he catches beatings for returning. He sees jail time. In the cells he hears more. From convicts whose pathways chance avenues of ill repute where, as Crick sees it, armless boys may be forced to tarry.

Crick slips down these outlets, himself becoming a wanderer of the underbelly, where he takes odd employments and keeps company with tattoo artists who convince him the drawings now on his skin would render his image unrecognizable from the Crick of the past, and he allows his face and arms to be inked to their now remarkable appearance.

His journeys bring him to dilapidated towns. Broken villages littered with skeletons. Reminders of his family's falling.

But it is not all bad. There are moments of glory as he traipses the earth, as he pauses and sees in distances before him citrus orchards toasting in the bake of sunlight, the perfume of them bright and tangy, soporific and clean. Or further south in his wanderings, into the mountains of Mexico, where ramshackle houses made from cinder blocks and blankets sit in the shadow of Cola de Caballo—Horse Tail Falls—and the sound of the rushing waters fills his ears like white noise as the residents speak their music-shaped language in response to his continuing query, "A boy with no arms?"

And Crick has never found him.

Now there is Crick in the cage with a fragment of skull in his grip, but who the skull belongs to is unknown, and all the armless boys who Crick found in his journeys were the sons of other men. Sad boys with vacant faces straining in dust-flavored dwellings.

That mission, to find his child, was abandoned. Instead, Crick decided to spread word of the terrors of the mother-fucking sharks, but so often his labors found him in situations similar to this.

Crick sits on the hard bed in his cell. He stares at the skull. He wonders if he'll ever see his boy again.

The thunder starts.

V

V

Kinky Pete rushed in bleeding, and Mom watched him absently as he fidgeted a wet washrag from a bucket and began to dab his face.

"What happened to you?" she asked.

"Nothing worth mentioning," he told her.

Mom thought: Nothing with men ever is.

She thought: Look at him with his cut. Damn sad. I've seen him shoot men dead and now he bleeds like a child. I've seen so many silly men. This one. His blood caught in the rag from the water bucket. Was it preordained that I'd be so inundated by puny men? In the pattern of the stars is it organized that my acquaintances with the opposite sex would be bungled? I find them foolish and haphazard, and yet physically I crave them. Perhaps that is the evilest side of my coin. I wish I was as those other women who find breasts and hips mesmerizing, but I can't sway myself in that direction. In my memory my father is feeble, but my mother was absent, and perhaps that's the saddest act of all—to run like a coward from a duty you've gestated. Father was a drunk, but he was there: in the morning light of the kitchen with a sundae bowl of bourbon to 'warm up his bones,' and he never did foul by me sexually, though I'm certain most who smelled his breath figured him a daughter toucher, but in my mind the tragedy of his self-driven destruction was the great undoer of my opinion of him. How can a creature's prime motivation be to poison itself? All he did was drink and hope to drink again. Even when he got ill off it, and had to hide from the sun, deep in whatever shade he could find with his head wrapped in wet cloth, he would beg me to fetch him whisky to alleviate his malaise and the excruciating moroseness of it, and that always further puzzled me: it was like trying to heal a burn with more fire. And that's what he was: a wound that wanted to be wounded. Here, this Kinky Pete, this face bleeding into a wet rag, here I find it paltry and clumsy, but I get it. Whatever secret situation caused the abrasion matters not. What matters is he's aiming to quell the ache with a sane method. I'd say "Daddy, just wait it out. Sit in the dark. I'll bring you cool water," and he'd laugh and say, "Why wait for what's coming anyhow?" And perhaps there was some logic in that. There never passed a day I didn't see him drinking. Eight in the morning or eight at night: is there much difference?

"He's an odd one."

Mom looked up, confused.

"But he can't hurt no one where we got him," said Pete, and Mom knew he meant the stranger. Pete took the blood-colored rag from his cheek, lowered his face to hers and asked, "Think it needs stitches?"

She surveyed the gash and could see clotted fat hanging limp and yellow at the edges. "Probably," she said, and Pete nodded.

"Figures," he said, and he turned and tossed the bloody rag back into the water bucket, stomped to the front door, threw it open and then banged it shut as he disappeared into the street.

Was there much difference? I don't drink, so maybe I don't know. I have drank, but not like that. I have tasted wine and I have felt it change me, but not like that. He would go from sick to swell in a swallow and a half, and he'd sing those foolish songs with a smile on his face, made up things that he pretended were real, the lyrics all rhyming and he'd pause for me to finish the couplets—

The first thing in gumbo is?

MOTHERFUCKING SHARKS

Roux
Which is basically a Cajun?
Stew
And the opposite of false is?
True
And the opposite of old is?
New

And he could go on that way for hours with his sundae bowl that he always drank from, and when I asked him why he'd say, "Because I love ice cream."

Fine. Ice cream. The thing that killed him. His smell changing and his skin turning yellow. A real man. Like all the men. Like the one today. Drawn on like a coloring book. Playing with toys. A real man. Shouting make believe stories on the street corner certain that everyone wanted to listen. Because he is a man.

Then the thunder starts.

Mom goes to the door and opens it. She steps onto the porch. In the distance she can see the white lightning coughing fits behind the jagged-peaked mountains, the sillhouettes of them more dramatic in the dark of the oncoming storm.

She thinks: Storm.

She thinks: Just like children.

She thinks: Ice cream.

Mom goes to the cupboard where Kinky Pete keeps the bourbon and plucks a bottle from the shelf. She goes to her room. At the foot of her bed, a trunk. Inside the trunk, her father's sundae bowl.

She thinks: All the same.

She thinks: Nothing but children.

She thinks: I'll take it to him.

Mom makes her way back on to the porch, down the few steps and into the single, proper street of the town.

She thinks: When I first came here there was one house made from mold-freckled timber.

She thinks: It's not where I want it, but it's getting there.

Mom had come to the town after her father died with an aunt who she met only once before her father's funeral. She was a baldheaded woman who wore a black bandana on her skull and smoked cigarettes and played harmonica. They had driven there by donkey-dragged wagon, and when they reached the house the aunt halted the donkey, said, "There you go," and looked out at nothing.

"There I go what?" asked Mom.

The aunt took one long drag on her cigarette, and Mom could hear the paper and tobacco burning to ash, turning to smoke. The aunt lunged the smoke, her face going tight as she breathed deep the air. She exhaled. She pointed at the house. "Get on up there," she said, "knock on that door," her words stained gray with the escaping smoke, "tell 'em what's brought you here."

Mom thought a moment. "You brought me here," she said.

Her aunt shook her head, "I mean your pa," she said, "dead as they come," she smoked again, "buried in the dirt." She nodded. "Tell 'em that and they'll take you in."

Mom looked at the sad little house. It looked like a good rain would wash it away. "And you?" she asked her aunt without looking at her, because she was old enough to figure the answer.

"Well," said the aunt, "I'll be back from time to time to check."

Mom looked at her. The aunt smiled guiltily. Some people are so worthless, they don't bother hiding their lies.

The aunt helped Mom pull her trunk from the wagon, but she did not help her drag it to the house. "Go and knock," she said, "they'll help you carry it in."

Mom nodded, walked toward the door. The aunt drove on before she'd even gotten there to knock.

Mom thinks: That house was empty.

She thinks: Was probably always empty.

She thinks: And she probably thought I'd die in it.

She remembered knocking and knocking again. She knocked and knocked again. It was summer and the sun shone so bright the light of the world seemed false, and the shadows of all things were darker than midnight, and young Mom sat sweating on that porch of that busted house trying to shade her face with her hand, and she waited until the sun sank away from noon and into evening, and she watched it half itself with the horizon and watched it slip away like an orange ghost, the sky's blue hue fading into nighttime's navy. She knocked again, then sat on the trunk with her knees pulled to her chin, terrified of the noises and the stars and the moon, and annoyed at the mosquitos who sank their poisonous suckers in her. She swatted herself pink. She itched herself awake, watching the moon trace the sky.

In the morning, the dew made her dress sticky.

She knocked on the door again. She knocked again.

She was tired and angry from being tired, and she decided she would no longer follow the etiquette taught to her. She turned the doorknob and went inside. It was as she feared. The house was entirely empty.

Mom thinks: I was only a child.

She thinks: But that childhood didn't last long.

"Wake up," Mom says.

She stands in front of Crick's cell, holds the bourbon bottle in one hand and the sundae bowl in the other.

Crick pulls his eyes open. His slumber breaks oddly. He shakes his head. "Storms always do it," he says, "I love to sleep through the rain."

Mom nods. "It's coming," she says, "you said it would," she pours the sundae bowl full of bourbon and walks to the bars. "Thirsty?" she says.

Crick nods. He stands and goes to her. He takes the sundae bowl from her and contemplates it. "I'd rather it be ice cream," he says and sips at it gingerly.

Mom smiles. She sets the bottle on the ground. In doing so, she sees the shattered skull bits. "What happened here?" she asks.

Crick sips his bourbon. "Ask that Kinky Pete," he says, and Mom nods because now she knows.

She looks about. She sees Crick's satchel. "You know," she says, "I can juggle too." She takes the skulls from the bag. "But I can only do three," she says. She takes a skull in each hand and lets the third rest on her right wrist. Crick watches her nervously.

Mom jerks her right arm toward the ceiling and the skull lifts from her wrist into the air. It begins to drop and she launches the skull from her left hand, catches the falling skull and tosses up the third. Her form is sloppy, but Crick watches her work the skulls from hand to hand, Mom's face pinched with concentration. She catches them and holds them a moment against her. "Tada," she says.

"Bravo," says Crick.

"I could never do four though," she says.

"Neither can I," he says, "I just do two with each hand."

Mom thinks a moment on this. "Is that how it's done?" she asks.

"It is," he says.

"Forgive me if I don't try," she says.

Crick smiles. "I'd actually rather you didn't."

Mom looks then at the skulls. "That's right," she says, "your family."

"That's right," says Crick.

Mom places the skulls back in the satchel. "And do people believe that?" she asks, "when you tell them?"

"Not usually," Crick says.

"And the sharks?"

"The motherfucking sharks," says Crick.

"Yes," says Mom, "the motherfucking sharks." She laughs. "Do people believe about them?"

"Rarely," says Crick.

"But you tell it anyway?"

Crick nods. He sips his drink. "You ever seen a boy with no arms?" he asks.

Mom looks at him oddly. "Is this a kind of riddle?" she asks.

Crick laughs. "Maybe," he says. "But if it is, I'm living it."

They are silent a moment. Thunder can be heard. But, another noise as well. Hollering. Shouting of some sort. The door flings open.

Scraw walks in with his hands on his head. Kinky Pete walks behind him. His pistol is drawn and his left hand holds a rag against his busted face.

"God damn it," hollers Kinky Pete. He looks at Mom. He looks at Crick. He holsters his pistol and opens Crick's cell with a key. "Well," he says, shoving Scraw in with Crick. "You were right," he says to Crick.

Crick laughs.

Mom looks at all the men. "Right about what?" she asks.

Pete just looks at her. He grits his teeth. He dabs his wound. "That stew," he yells, "it was not mule."

VI

IV

Kinky Pete walked the street repulsed at his anger because his anger made him throw the skull, birthed his need for stitches. There's not a person alive who's not phenomenal at hurting themselves. But Kinky Pete was better than most. He cussed himself as he dragged down the street to see Bark.

"You're a foolish piece of shit wrapped in the disguise of human flesh," he said, "throwing tantrums like a baby."

At Bark and Scraw's, Pete banged the door, the deep thud of his fist against the broad portal humming low in the night. "Bark," he hollered, "I'm cut and need sewing on."

The door did not open, but Scraw answered from inside, "Bark's sleeping." That was the extent of Scraw's offering on the matter. Night's silence came on again.

"Well," said Pete, "wake him up."

Silence.

Pete again banged the door, but no answer came.

"Scraw," he screamed, "I'm bleeding. Wake Bark. Tell him I need stitched up."

Silence.

Pete's patience fizzled out quick. He knelt to lift the door, but it was locked. "Scraw," he yelled, "Scraw, open up."

Scraw hollered back, "I can't."

Pete walked to the side of the building. Yellow light glowed from a window, and Pete perched on his tip toes to peek inside. He couldn't believe what he saw. He went back to the the door, and banged it again.

He screamed, "Scraw," and banged the door. He screamed,

"Scraw," again. "I looked in your window," he said. "I saw the damn mule."

Then the thunder starts.

Scraw says in a limp tone, "I can't believe what I've done."

Pete puzzles at this, "Open up," he says, "what are you talking about?"

Pete listens as Scraw keys the lock open from inside. He steps back from the door as it raises to reveal Scraw who stands aside the still-living Murm, petting the mule's mane. "I couln't kill it," Scraw says.

Pete nods. "Fine," he says, "where's Bark?"

Scraw leans his shoulder against the mule. "Bark wanted me to kill the mule, but I couldn't bring myself to do it."

"Fine," says Pete, "but where is he?"

"He was pushing me," says Scraw, "or," Scraw scratches his head, "I sure like this mule."

"Dammit, Scraw, don't make me ask again."

Scraw looks at nothing. "I don't know," he says, "because I'm not sure how it works. My only memory of my mother is her telling me how the sunshine became the flowers, and she said 'every time you pick a flower, it's like holding a ray of sun,' because she said that sun was how flowers made their food. I dropped bowls of Bark to the prisoner and to the poor families, but I don't know if that means they're part Bark or if Bark's part them, and what I didn't drop off is in the pot on the stove." Scraw points to a large steel pot that is streaked with brown stew down its sides. "And the bone part of Bark is out back in the bone pile." Scraw looks at Pete. "Do you want me to bring that part back in here?"

Kinky Pete draws his gun. He says, "Nope, best to come with me," and he leads Scraw to the cell where Crick is held captive and deposits him there.

On Pete's way home with Mom, it begins to rain.

Rain, Rain, Rain

This is the part where it rains. It will rain so good, you will go get lines from it tattooed on your body and every time it is raining outside you will find strangers in the rain, going to them while holding an umbrella, and you will look them in the eyes and say, "How about this weather?" and they will say, "I know," and then you will show them the tattooed line from this book that made you think anew about rain, and their eyes will smile at you, just the two of you beneath your umbrella, locked in the magic of the words on the subject of rain as inked on your body by a tattoo artist who probably likes girl on girl porn.

Mom is home with her face against the window. Kinky Pete is home on his porch playing with his pistol. Crick and Scraw are in the cell. Murm stands inside the slaughterhouse in front of the door swishing his tail watching the puddles grow.

Armies of drops fall, swelling the streets with impromptu rivers. The roofs cast sheets of rain from their lips like waterfalls. The thunder booms. The lightning strobes. The music of the falling rain hisses.

Rain According To Pete

I don't know how it gets in the sky. I'm serious. The rain. They probably taught me at some point, but I didn't pay attention, because my back always aches so much I don't pay attention to school-type things, but I do know enough to know it starts off as water and gets turned to clouds, and that the clouds get too heavy, you can tell by the look of them, and then it just falls. It's a storm. But it can rain with the sun out. Used to we'd say, when it rained and was sunny, that the devil was beating his wife, but I have no idea where that saying came from. Sayings are always stupid things. I had a Mexican aunt couldn't speak English, and she used to say to me, whenever I hurt myself, "Sana sana colita de rana," which meant, "heal heal little frog tail," and her saying it was supposed to take away the pain, but I'm not certain how, and my uncle used to say, "A monkey in a dress is still a monkey," but he never saw a monkey in his whole life, so I don't know where he came up with that.

Rain, Rain, Rain

Rain, Rain, Rain, Rain, Rain, Rain, Rain, Rain, Rain, Rain,
Rain, Rain, Rain, Rain, Rain, Rain, Rain, Rain, Rain, Rain,
Rain, Rain, Rain, Rain, Rain, Rain, Rain, Rain, Rain, Rain,
Rain, Rain, Rain, Rain, Rain, Rain, Rain, Rain, Rain, Rain,
Rain, Rain, Rain, Rain, Rain, Rain, Rain, Rain, Rain, Rain,
Rain, Rain, Rain, Rain, Rain, Rain, Rain, Rain, Rain, Rain,
Rain, Rain, Rain, Rain, Rain, Rain, Rain, Rain, Rain, Rain,
Rain, Rain, Rain, Rain, Rain, Rain, Rain, Rain, Rain, Rain,
Rain, Rain, Rain, Rain, Rain, Rain, Rain, Rain, Rain, Rain,
Rain, Rain, Rain, Rain, Rain, Rain, Rain, Rain, Rain, Rain,
Rain, Rain, Rain, Rain, Rain, Rain, Rain, Rain, Rain, Rain,
Rain, Rain, Rain, Rain, Rain, Rain, Rain, Rain, Rain, Rain,
Rain, Rain, Rain, Rain, Rain, Rain, Rain, Rain, Rain, Rain,
Rain, Rain, Rain, Rain, Rain, Rain, Rain, Rain, Rain, Rain,
Rain, Rain, Rain, Rain, Rain, Rain, Rain, Rain, Rain, Rain,
Rain, Rain, Rain, Rain, Rain, Rain, Rain, Rain, Rain, Rain,
Rain, Rain, Rain, Rain, Rain, Rain, Rain, Rain, Rain, Rain,
Rain, Rain, Rain, Rain, Rain, Rain, Rain, Rain, Rain, Rain,
Rain, Rain, Rain, Rain, Rain, Rain, Rain, Rain, Rain, Rain,
Rain, Rain, Rain, Rain, Rain, Rain, Rain, Rain, Rain, Rain,
Rain, Rain, Rain, Rain, Rain, Rain, Rain, Rain, Rain, Rain,
Rain, Rain, Rain, Rain, Rain, Rain, Rain, Rain, Rain, Rain,
Rain, Rain, Rain, Rain, Rain, Rain, Rain, Rain, Rain, Rain,
Rain, Rain, Rain, Rain, Rain, Rain, Rain, Rain, Rain, Rain,
Rain, Rain, Rain, Rain, Rain, Rain, Rain, Rain, Rain, Rain,
Rain, Rain, Rain, Rain, Rain, Rain, Rain, Rain, Rain, Rain,
Rain, Rain, Rain, Rain, Rain, Rain, Rain, Rain, Rain, Rain,
Rain, Rain, Rain, Rain, Rain, Rain, Rain, Rain, Rain, Rain,

Rain, Rain, Rain, Rain, Rain, Rain, Rain, Rain, Rain, Rain,
Rain, Rain, Rain, Rain, Rain, Rain, Rain, Rain, Rain, Rain,
Rain, Rain, Rain, Rain, Rain, Rain, Rain, Rain, Rain, Rain,
Rain, Rain, Rain, Rain, Rain, Rain, Rain, Rain, Rain, Rain,
Rain, Rain, Rain, Rain, Rain, Rain, Rain, Rain, Rain, Rain,
Rain, Rain, Rain, Rain, Rain, Rain, Rain, Rain, Rain, Rain,
Rain, Rain, Rain, Rain, Rain, Rain, Rain, Rain, Rain, Rain,
Rain, Rain, Rain, Rain, Rain, Rain, Rain, Rain, Rain, Rain,
Rain, Rain, Rain, Rain, Rain, Rain, Rain, Rain, Rain, Rain,
Rain, Rain, Rain, Rain, Rain, Rain!

Rain According to Scraw

Maybe it's like God crying because I killed Bark. Not every time, but this time. I think God exists. I might be going to Hell. The guy in the cell with me definitely is. I'm thirsty. I'm gonna hold my hand out the window and catch some of God's tears and drink them. If the water I catch is salty, well the rain is God's tears for certain.

Rain in Various Languages

German: Regnen
Spanish: Lluvia
French: Pluie
Italian: Pioggia
Pig Latin: Ainray

Rain According to Crick

Fuck the rain, and fuck this weird guy with his hand out the window.

Rain According to You

_____

_____

_____

_____

_____

_____

_____

_____

_____

_____

_____

_____

_____

_____

_____

_____

Rain According to Mom

Because he liked ice cream. That's why he drank liquor from a sundae bowl. I bet it even made sense to him once upon a time. Or, maybe the first time he said it. The first time he said it, it probably got him a laugh, and after that he just said it all the time, but I never laughed at it. I'd just look at him like, "Why?" What he needed was water. It's what we all need. Not this much. The juggler, he was right about the rain, but I just can't believe he's right about the sharks. He doesn't seem crazy when you talk to him, but he doesn't seem honest either. Maybe he tells people about the motherfucking sharks coming out after the rain for the same reason my father said he drank because he liked ice cream. Maybe. Somehow. Somewhere. It worked for him. The story about his family too. Maybe in some towns, the people go in for the theatrics of it. They like the drama of his past's misery, and they celebrate his act and treat him as a renowned performer.

The Rain Stops

Here is how it starts: with a whisper, a hiss. A shallow spray the scent of fresh. It comes first as pure calm. The tree limbs that fooled in the breeze go serious, fall still, and the world seems paused in anticipation. But in that hallowed still there seems a promise. The nutrition of nature is imminent. The ashy second skin of the world sat dry will be washed gone, and dragged on makeshift currents to conclusions only God can perceive.

In the town, the hush of the coming storm dwindles, eaten by the noise of that which is certain, and with silence's tapering, residents seek refuge in dwellings ill-equipped for flood—the security provided by them more mental than actual—and they hold their breaths and seek their misplaced religion, hiding behind verses their forefathers died clucking in battle so that their descendants might lead softer lives—the byproduct of their easy living ironically the cause of their failing beliefs.

But here in this fear of God's hammer, a re-awakening of those cultural touchstones. Soul-shaped hands seek heaven-shaped promises to hold and hold onto, even as the storm douses the streets until they bulge like blisters—the girth of them puny against the eternity of the flood.

Take a coin from your pocket and pour a gallon on it.

Take a coin from your pocket and drop it into a gallon.

Take a coin.

Here the homes wiggle and sway with wind. Here the roofs leak streams from low holes into buckets that miserably perform.

Children hold their mothers. Wives hold their husbands. Husbands hold their breaths.

This storm is a carbon copy.

A carbon copy of prior storms.

Magically, no one dies in the dread of it. The weather seems aware of the townsfolk's limitations.

The relentlessness of it relents.

Family members cross themselves as the deluge dwindles.

The sun.

The sun can be seen.

Behind smoke-shaped clouds that scrape open like lace.

They're alive.

The storm did not kill them.

VII

IV

The sun plows the clouds to nothing. The blue of sky like a sheet of life the fiery coin of the sun just clings to. It is there, casting rays that warm the puddles which sit stagnant and bored in their sockets, children stomping them and ladies looking into them at their reflections.

Here are the people of the town rejoicing at the storm's quelling. Here they are in the sun of the day. The mud of the street clumps to the soles of their shoes, stains the hems of their slacks and dresses, and babies are set in it to wallow like pigs as their parents bare thrive-stained smiles—beaming at their ability to outlive the disastrous weather that had held them tight in their homes the way envelopes hold letters.

Mom stands on her porch in the fresh morning air, and Pete, so pleased at the jolly figures in the roads, plucks his revolver from its holster and fires bullets at the sky, "Can't kill us," he says to God, and then all the men with guns fire heaven-headed rounds, and someone brings a bourbon bottle into the street, and they open it and pass it around like a conch shell and whoever has it says some flavor-laced toast about Jesus or their mothers and then drinks from the thing until every willing party in the town has espoused their happiness and lipped the mouth of the thing, making themselves silly with liquor.

A free-for-all ensues. Guilty pleasures abound. Men kiss women, kiss men. Babies are held up by their ankles and swung, and their laughter emits like helium-drenched music. Souls prance in the shape of smiles. Kittens are given milk.

Murm wanders blinking his one eye at the wildness of it, and girls tie flowers to his tail.

Scraw watches from the jail cell window, "That's my mule," he hollers.

"The mule is his own thing," says Crick. He grins blackly at the affronted joy. He knows it will soon perish.

In the puddles that glimmer with sun, the evil things are hatching.

In sun-glittering puddles the sharks are forming.

In the shiny puddles.

The puddles—like mirrors toward the sky.

Look now close at them. Here are the things to see:

1. You in it, a reflection or refraction depending on the stillness of the water.

2. The murk of the muddy slop or the shape of the road beneath the inches of wet depending on the stillness of the water.

3. The disturbances. Tiny tickles of motion. Like mosquitos at first, beating their wings. But something more. It steadies. Outline of shark. So small you could swallow them with just their skin slicked by the puddles they're pulled from. And what then would occur to you? The motherfucking shark's progress so deep in its operation cannot be stopped by normal means, and the expansion of the organism—formulated by the blackest deceit of physics, organics, and chemistry—would continue, and you'd feel it first as an ache in your belly that would broaden like a rage or fire and maintain its trajectory of expanse until the shark gained full form, and that growth of it, the swiftest of maturations, would sever your figure beneath the force of it, your body blasting open as gore and sludge, the muck of you draping away from the gray-bodied being that would swim out of you whilst gnashing its teeth and thrashing its fins, breathing the flavor of you through its gills that would glisten with your blood.

It is Mom who spots first the trembling puddles. At first

it seems joyous to her. The shiny surfaces giggling with light.

But then she thinks: I'd rather it be ice cream.

That thought, that statement from the wanderer, festers.

Maybe it's not a lie.

And further the puddles are disturbed, as though an earthquake shakes them, but the world is otherwise still.

"Maybe," hollers Mom above the drone of the people celebrating the end of the wicked storm, "we should move this party inside."

But, it is too late.

On the ground, near a puddle, its face the smell of chocolate, a toddler toddles.

See this, friend: eyes green, cheeks alight with joy. Blonde hair only ever so slightly feathered by breeze. A giggle. A tummy laugh. You ever touched a toddler's tummy? It feels like suede-wrapped heaven. It smells like milk and hugs and handshakes from God. You see this little boy? This little white boy? If it hurts you more to see a black boy die, then make him black in your mind, I don't care what it looks like so long as you're uncomfortable. Instead, reader, do this. Picture for me, if you will, the child you love the most. Hold it in your head. Dress it with the form you'd least like to see killed. In this way, we have always been a team. I tell you a thing, but you spin it real in your head. So, I won't tell you everything. Hell, make it a girl. Make it your own. Give me a child. Put it in your mind. Put it by a puddle. Put joy in its heart. I'm going to fuck it up. I'm going to unleash a magical shark on it. I'm going to turn that precious thing into a bucket of death shaped the way that hurts you most. Put that fucking child by that fucking puddle and let me kill the fuck out of it. I will strip its skin from its body, toss chunks of it at you like strips of bacon. Your baby. Make the fucking baby. I want to kill the fucking baby you've made in your mind. Is it there? Is it the baby?

Now, up comes the shark.

Now listen, I'm serious here, I'm willing to sacrifice my spot in Heaven to make you feel bad while reading this. I'll quit drinking forever tomorrow, and I won't jerk off to amateur porn anymore—you know the kind that's been stolen and where the women look embarrassed and the men look eager and the light is yellow and you can nearly smell the sin—but it won't matter anymore, because after I kill this toddler out of your imagination, God will think me reprehensible. I want this to all occur inside of you. We're a team, okay? We're gonna kill this little kid together.

Kill this kid with me.

Put it in your mind and let's kill it.

Just you and me.

Just you and me and our imaginations.

Just two people. Taking a kid and killing it in our hearts.

It's not real.

It's just.

Let's take this kid. This cute little kid. It's by the puddle. And in that puddle is something dark.

The child is innocent. The shark is heinous. Teeth. Teeth. Teeth.

Look at a baby's hand. It's so soft.

Look at a shark's mouth. All those teeth, so sharp.

Take that soft little hand, with those soft little fingers. Piggies. Piggies.

Sing: this little piggy went to market, this little piggy stayed home.

God, I'm gonna fucking put those cute little fingers in that fucking shark's mouth. God, it will be fucked up. I'm gonna drag them over the teeth. Oh, shit, they will not stand a chance.

Hahaha. Look at the baby's face. It's fucking crying.

There's blood everywhere.

It's trying to suck its thumb.

Hey, dumbass, thumb's gone.

I fed it to a fucking shark.

Hahahahhahahahahahahahahahaahaa.
Oh.
It bites the kid again.
Oh, man.
These motherfucking sharks are crazy.

VIII

Kinky Pete bolts into the sheriff's office and races to the open cell alongside Crick and Scraw's. He gets inside pulling the cage door closed behind him. "What the fuck is happening?" he screams.

"I take it you've met the motherfucking sharks?"

Scraw is screaming, looking out the window at the sharks that are destroying the people of the town. Biting and thrashing, spraying the street with blood.

A nurse shark rams its way into the jail. It slams frantically against the cage bars, trying to bite at Pete. Pete cowers, his hands over his face. Scraw cries hysterically. Crick picks at his teeth.

Pete pulls his pistol and fires four shots at the shark. The bullets pass straight through it.

"No use," says Crick, "only harpoons kill them."

Pete looks at Crick. "Why?" he asks.

"Because they are magical, flying sharks and that's how they die," he says. "Pierce 'em with a harpoon and they burst into flames and the only thing that remains of them is their jaws that drop to the ground from their burning mouths," says Crick. "I've felled loads of them and have the mementos tied to my wagon just outside."

Pete looks sadly at his pistol. "I don't believe it," he says.

"Like with the stew?" says Crick.

Pete looks deeply now into Crick's eyes.

"Go fetch me a harpoon," says Crick, "and I'll show you."

Pete looks at the nurse shark just outside the cage. It

gnashes and thrashes. Pete thinks. "Maybe," he says, "we could send out Scraw."

Scraw screams a crazy-girl-shaped holler.

"Shut up," says Crick, and he kicks Scraw, and Scraw hunches toward the floor and screams even louder.

Crick looks at Pete. "I don't think he has the nerves for it," he says, but the noise of Scraw endures.

Pete nods agreement, shakes his head at the commotion. "He's a killer anyhow," he says. He takes aim at Scraw's skull, pulls the pistol's trigger and a shot erupts and Scraw's head oozes open and he goes quiet, his body limping to the floor where a puddle of blood smears out around him. Pete holsters the gun. "How long does it last?" Pete asks pointing at the nurse shark.

Crick shrugs. "All of today," he says. "Maybe some of tomorrow."

The two men go to their respective bunks. They both sit. They quietly watch the shark.

Pete takes a plug of tobacco from his pocket and mouths a chew of it.

Outside the sharks charge the townsfolk into terrified clumps, the bulk of them like wads of fear, pock-marked with terror-stricken eyes. These cowering clusters breathe screams as a single organism would, low-droning shouts blend with pitch-pointed shrieks, and the music of it bellows as a bagpiper tuning may, only the lunging attacks of sharks plunging into the mess of folks like grey and toothed fists pop off the steadiness of the choir by subtracting voices from its congregation, and the strikes change the musicality or add to it depending—the wayward tones flittered with blood and the ache-noise of someone's dying or dismemberment and the sea salt smell of the shark-shaped mastication.

Pete: That one looks mean.
Crick: They're all mean.

An athletic-looking boy races down the road pursued by a hammerhead with evil-fuck eyes. Make believe you are the camera. The boy races toward you.

Now you are the camera above. The shark is after the boy.

You are beside the shark. Its dorsal fin whistles against the air as the fish races on.

Beside the boy. He huffs and pants, his feet skipping across the gravel, the sound of match sticks against striker pads.

Again above. The shark gains ground.

And in front again. The boy so close the fear on his face repulses you, the skin around his eyes red as fire, and then the hammerhead thrashes down upon the boy's collar, and the two lift above your line of sight until the last you see of the boy is his sneaker cracking your camera lens.

You are now beside them both, high in the air, the boy's neck gushing blood, vomit tossing from his mouth, tears streaking his face, and the shark is thrashing.

Pete: Know any jokes?
    Crick: No.

A father and daughter race toward home. She is too slow and he raises her to his hip and makes his legs run faster than they ever have. They burn, his legs, but not like fire. It is as though his muscles are filled with saltwater instead of blood, and aching from the corrosion of trying to manipulate that liquid into fuel.

He loves his daughter.

She is his only living kin.

He didn't know his people, and he just witnessed his wife's annihilation, her body scraped open and emptied of its mess—globules and morsels and smidgens and niggles. Things like red marbles slick with oil and pink balloons deformed by age, just quaking from her walloped-around body.

He can't let his daughter die.

He doesn't look behind him.

He knows they are near, and he begs his legs, his lungs, his heart, through some physical prayer the mind makes to the body, to move faster still, to thwart the smarting back to corners and un-anguish in any way imaginable and give him more.

His daughter faints from fear in his clutch.

He makes it to the porch.

To the door.

Reaches for the knob.

Tries to turn it, but it is locked.

Terrified, he turns.

A great white is upon him and the cast-wide mouth sprawls

its shiv-sculpted teeth at him, and in his last act, just a cowardly reflex really, he lifts his daughter at the shark, stuffing her body into its jaws, but the monster is so mighty, it bites them both in two.

Pete: There's an alcoholic in a potato sack race.
    Crick: Is this the joke?
    Pete: Yeah.

An aging lady holds a crucifix in front of her.

Her entire frame is trembling, her wrinkly little face like a frightened prune.

A bull shark takes its teeth to her leg. She brings the cross down upon it over and over again. It does nothing.

She hears her flesh tear open—like a bed sheet being ripped at—and she just dies from the shock of it.

Pete: He's hopping down the track in the lead, and he sees a bar.

A blind man stands still with his arms outstretched.

A gray whirr scurries by him.

Now his hands are gone and blood gushes from his wrists and his face looks confused—his impotent eyes as wide open as walnuts.

He thinks, 'I'm so far ahead, I'll just hop in here for a quick one.'

Murm walks the street unfazed.

He whips his tail all casual.

He blinks at the beastly bits left behind by the sharks.

Steps over the bones and severed limbs, setting his hooves instead into puddles of blood and muck, shredded flesh and burst-open bladders. Shit and piss. Puss and ooze. Guts caught in potholes like buckets of chum.

Murm finds an onion cart overturned in the road.

He eats one of the maroon-skinned vegetables.

Chews patiently as sharks whiz around him.

He hops up to the bar and says, 'Shot of whisky, please.'

Mom screams, "Follow me," and leads three girls in an odd, stumbling progression through the dregs of the mudded-up street, now slippery with blood and threads of flung human flesh.

In Mom's mind, a fear tone drones, the smack of shark jaws on human flesh providing a percussion ill-timed. Alongside that, the noise of their steps in the soup of the road, the plunking and slurping of their course illustrating their slow, steady migration away from the assemblages of herded townsfolk—in their ill-fated congregations just delaying for death—and toward a hopeful sanctuary of a storm cellar behind a pale-yellow house.

The smell of warm puddles, warm blood, and salt water. The smell of the mud, the fear, the sun.

The three girls shriek like steam fleeing teapots.

They are a chain of humans, fastened by hands.

They are all so terrified, you cannot tell the true age of them, but they seem to descend in maturity, starting with Mom.

A requiem shark sweeps down from the skies at the weakest link of them, shanking her away from the chain of females fleeing.

And then there were three.

Miraculously, mud-streaked, blood-soaked, the now young-est holding still the detached arm of the one they lost—the arm dangling queerly and flexing with nerves—they make it to the cellar.

"You girls first," says Mom, and she pushes them down the steps.

Bartender just looks at him.

A whitetip is upon Mom. It has gripped her thigh through her denim dress just as Mom was about to descend into the cellar. She fights it, driving her elbows down against the dorsal fin, jabbing fists at the gills.

It was the nose she should have aimed for.

Realizing she can't defeat it, won't shake from its grip, Mom slams shut the cellar door, clamps the pad lock of it shut—all the time screams of the girls below ringing hot in her mind.

Once locked, a lucky strike is landed. Mom puts a fist down into the face of the shark, and the thing lets loose a moment, shakes its head.

Mom takes advantage.

She turns.

Her leg is messed with wound, panging wildly, but she flees.

On bungled limbs she runnels forth, murking her way across the flood-gutted street and beyond the town's perimeter into the adjacent spare-grass lands now swampy with standing wet, dotted green by patches of swaying St. Augustine grass.

'I can't serve you,' the bartender says.

There is no more aggressive a shark than the tiger.

The great white might be king, but the tiger is the assassin.

The young are striped, hence the name.

Their noses blunted, their teeth wildly asymmetrical and serrated, their appetites undiscerning so they'll eat the flesh of anything.

They can live fifty years, growing up to fourteen feet long and weigh on average one-hundred pounds per foot.

They swim in shoals, but will hunt alone.

If they see movement, they attack, and they don't let go.

See now the tiger shark above the town where the hollers of those being attacked has quelled to murmurs, whispers, tones?

You see it, and it sees Mom.

It swims now toward her, and she has stumbled to a stop, falling upon soft earth where she pants for breath.

She rolls onto her back, hoists herself to her elbows to look at her town now waylaid by the vicious, impossible creatures.

She sees it, the tiger.

It howls steadily toward her, but Mom has nothing left. She is leaked out through the wound on her thigh, which is now numbed by shock and no longer feels the squelch of shred but instead feels packed away beneath stacks of weights, and it is this weight that stills her. She is pale fatigue on the back of a wooden spoon. She is slow nothing in a pocket of put-away pants.

She thinks: I bet it is a man, this shark.

She thinks: I'll spread my legs at him.

With legs heaved open, Mom lays her head back, and a wild, electric lust spreads over her.

She thinks: We only die once.

She thinks: I will try to enjoy it.

She feels the force of the tiger's speed upon her like a wind, and then the beast traps her pussy in his jaws, driving her back into the mud, and she gives over the smooth surface of it, her path leaving a slug trail of blood and slick, and the shark shakes viciously, and Mom throws her head back in agony, her vision filled with endlessness of sky, and just before the tiger undoes her she thinks: Who will free them from the cellar?

'You're already half in the bag.'

The screams from the street have faded entirely. The sharks amass around the cells. They swim constantly at the bars. Some of the smaller ones make it through. Crick and Pete grab them by the tails and beat them on the floors until they are barely sharks anymore. Even after their skin has been scraped away, and they are essentially piles of organs and yuk, they live in an undead way, wriggling their battered bodies against the floor violently. Pete spits at them.

Pete: I can see the veins in them.

Crick: They'll be gone soon.

VIII 1/2

Pete wakes to find Crick staring at him. "What is it?" he asks.

"They're gone."

Pete pries himself off his bunk, shaking his body into some capable configuration, and he steps to his feet awkwardly, bumbling around with haphazard movement until he finds his balance. He puts his hands over his head. Yawns. Scratches his back. He looks around. He listens. "You sure?" he asks.

"Positive," says Crick. "Watched 'em vanish while you were sleeping."

Pete thinks. He smiles. He fishes the cell keys from his pants pocket, feeds them through the bars and awkwardly unlocks the cage. He pushes the door and it creaks rustily open. He steps out cautiously. It is ungracefully silent. He heads toward the door.

"Ain't you gonna let me out?" asks Crick.

Pete looks back at him. "Why would I?" he asks, and he walks to the doorway and out into the street.

Once he's gone, Crick produces a metal pick from beneath his tongue. He goes to the cell door and jimmies it open. He follows Pete out into the world.

Pete stands dumbfounded. The sun is high and angry, and the gore of the aftermath shines irrationally like a gem. There's a glimmer to the butchering. The puddles, the slick bones, the flung flesh, the wobbled away eyes.

Black birds are hoisted upon everything like flight-gifted rot, tearing scattered death into smaller bits which they fumble ineptly while seeking solitude from their brethren birds.

The homes and buildings, never entirely well put together, are busted and battered from the ungainly patterns of the sharks' feeding frenzies. Splinters of timber are tossed with the bone bits, the debris of destruction like a gravel of death.

Crick walks to his wagon and plucks a harpoon from the bunch of them. "Ain't a pretty sight is it?" he asks Pete whose back is to him.

Pete turns in awe. "How'd you get out?" he asks.

"Magic," says Crick.

Pete's eyes find the blade of the harpoon leveled at him.

He reaches for his pistol, but as he does, Crick flings the harpoon, and before Pete has unholstered the gun, he is impaled by the weapon, which lifts him from the ground and drives him back, stapling him against the wall of the sheriff's building, where he dangles by the heart upchucking blood down his chest.

Crick goes to him with a knife. "People like you," he says, "they don't ever listen."

IX

Howard and Gall sit in the living room playing checkers. It is a battered world, and family members falter. A woman is a woman if she says she is. A man, if he can prove it. Howard's father has been dead three years. His best friend Gall has been helping with the ranch. They are both fourteen, but markedly different. Gall knows horses, has big strong shoulders. Howard still chews his lip, would rather whittle than work.

Gall moves a piece. "King me," he says.

Howard's mother looks into the room. She sees the game at play. "Who's winning?" she asks. She had Howard when young and is still pristine. Her blonde hair is pulled behind her ears. She's been washing in the kitchen, and her white cotton blouse is tight on her breasts, near see-through where wet.

Howard looks at her. "Gall is," he says.

Gall looks at her. "Like always," he says.

She smiles at him and rubs her hands together. "You let me know when you're tired of that kid's game," she says.

"Why come?" asks Gall.

"Well," she says, "thought you and I might play something else."

It is as though Howard is not there entirely, and it has been this way for weeks. He's been listening to their fucking from his bedroom confusedly, and he has seen this foreplay banter displayed in front of him ad nauseum.

"I'm gonna go check the horses," Howard says, and he stands to leave the house.

"Ah, c'mon," says Gall. "You might still come back. Game's not over."

"We'll pick it up later," says Howard, "just leave the board as it is."

As Howard makes his way out of the house and onto the front porch, he hears his mom tell Gall, "Get your little ass in my bedroom, boy. I got something special for you."

Howard steps into the yard just in time to see the wayward traveler, who leads a one-eyed mule. The mule drags a wagon brimming with harpoons and nets, and shambling behind the rickety wooden carriage, on tethers of varying lengths, are the naked jaws of sharks, their multitudes of teeth chipping and chirping along the dirt. There is a music to it all, a sort of macabre waltz or a hysterical dirge. All percussion. All noise. Bloodcurdling. Amusing. Daffy. Absurd.

The traveler looks up, contemplates Howard. "What are the people here like?" he asks.

Howard thinks a moment. "They're motherfuckers," he says.

The traveler nods. "Then you'll need one of these," he says. He takes a harpoon from his wagon, walks it to Howard and sets it in his hands.

Howard is confused.

"You'll understand when the time comes," says the traveler. He smacks his mule's hindquarters and the mule drags forward.

Just as he's leaving, Howard sees, in the front seat of the wagon, sitting on a pillow, a decapitated head with a cut on its cheek.

ABOUT THE AUTHOR

Brian Allen Carr is the author of some motherfucking books, including *Short Bus* (Texas University Press), *Edie and the Low-Hung Hands* (Small Doggies Press), and *Vampire Conditions* (Holler Presents). His short fiction has appeared in *McSweeney's Small Chair, Hobart, Boulevard,* and other publications. He's also the winner of the inaugural Texas Observer Story Prize, judged by Larry McMurtry. Brian lives near the Texas/Mexico border, where sharks do occasionally rain from the sky.